This Little Tiger book belongs to:

_____

_____

_____

For Andrea & Claudia
— I.F.

For Mum & Dad, who helped
— J.T.

LITTLE TIGER PRESS
An imprint of Magi Publications
1 The Coda Centre, 189 Munster Road, London SW6 6AW
www.littletigerpress.com

First published in Great Britain 1999
This edition published 2005

The Very Lazy Ladybird

by Isobel Finn & Jack Tickle

LITTLE TIGER PRESS
London

This is the story of
a very lazy ladybird.

She liked to sleep all day . . .

and all night.

And because she slept
all day and all night,
this lazy ladybird didn't
know how to fly.

One day the lazy
ladybird wanted to
sleep somewhere else.
But what could she do
if she couldn't fly?

Then the lazy
ladybird had
a very good
idea.

she hopped into her pouch.

But the kangaroo liked to

JUMP!

"I can't sleep in here,"
cried the lazy ladybird.
"It's far too bumpy."

So when a tiger padded by . . .

she hopped on to his back.

But the tiger liked to

ROAR!

"I can't sleep here,"
said the lazy ladybird.
"It's far too noisy."

So when a crocodile swam by . . .

she hopped on to his tail.

But the crocodile liked to

SWISH

his tail in the water.

"I can't sleep here,"
said the lazy ladybird.
"I'll fall into the river!"

So when a monkey swung by . . .

she hopped on to her head.

But the monkey liked to

SWING

from branch to branch.

"I can't sleep here,"
said the lazy ladybird.
"I'm feeling dizzy."

So when a bear ambled by . . .

she hopped on to his ear.

But the bear liked to

SCRATCH!

"I can't sleep here,"
said the lazy ladybird.
"He'll never sit still."

So when a tortoise plodded by . . .

she hopped on to her shell.

But the tortoise liked to
S N O O Z E
in the sun.
"I can't sleep here,"
said the lazy ladybird.
"It's far too hot."

So when an elephant trundled by . . . .

she hopped on to his trunk.

"At last!" said
the lazy ladybird.
"I've found
someone
who doesn't . . .

But at that very moment . . . .

the elephant

So when an elephant trundled by . . .

she hopped on to his trunk.

"At last!" said
the lazy ladybird.
"I've found
someone
who doesn't . . .

jump . . .

But at that very moment . . .

the elephant

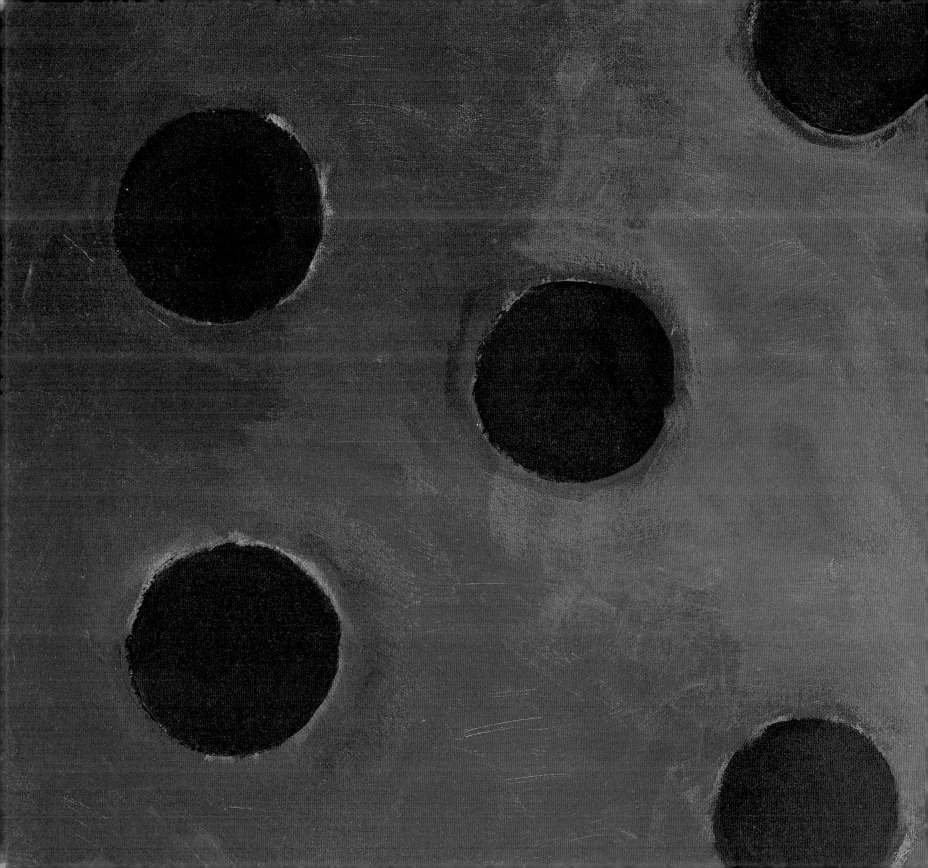

Spot more great books
from Little Tiger Press

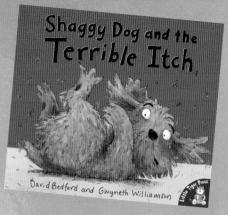

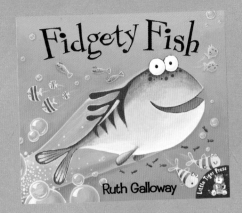

For information regarding the above titles or for
our catalogue, please contact us: Little Tiger Press

1 The Coda Centre

189 Munster Road

London SW6 6AW, UK

Tel: 020 7385 6333

Fax: 020 7385 7333

E-mail: info@littletiger.co.uk

www.littletigerpress.com